FOREVER COUSINS

Laurel Goodluck

Illustrated by **Jonathan Nelson**

Charlesbridge

AMANDA'S favorite color is purple.

KARA loves pink.

They agree that
sunflowers are beautiful,

powwow dancing is fun,

and chokecherry jam
on toast is the best.

Amanda declares that the new dolls
their magúu made should go everywhere
with them.

Kara decides that little cousin
Forrest is a bother.

And neither cousin can believe that Kara's
family is moving from the city to the Rez tomorrow.

Kara has a long,
bumpy ride ahead.
Cousin goodbyes are
bumpy, too.

"You'll see each other at the reunion next summer," says Kara's mama.

Amanda looks at her own mama and says, "That's a long time."

Kara's and Amanda's hearts are heavy
after their first month apart.
"I don't want to dance without Kara,"
Amanda whispers to her doll.

"How about some fry bread?" Kara's mama asks.

Kara hugs her doll and shakes her head.

The start of the school year means it's time to pick out a new lunch box!

Amanda calls Kara, saying, "I got a purple kitty lunch box."

And Kara tells Amanda about her pink
pony lunch box.

Kara ends the call and says to her doll,
"I wonder what my new school will be like."

In winter, Amanda finds puddles on the way home from school that make big splashes.

At home she discovers a postcard from Kara on the kitchen table.

Amanda reads about Kara sledding on the prairie and shows the postcard to her dad.

That spring, Kara wins the three-legged race and shows the prize to her dad.

"Do you think Amanda is having fun too?" asks Kara.

"Yes. I'm sure she is. She's probably finding the most eggs right now," says Dad.

Kara agrees and goes back to the Easter fun.

Finally it's summer again. Time for the family reunion! Butterflies bubble up in Amanda's belly as they pack her suitcase.

Dad fumbles with the GPS. Mama turns up her favorite song. Goodbye city, and hello road trip to the Rez!

The trip will take two days.
They cross the first state line,
and everyone shouts, "Woo-hoo!"

Kara's smile is as bright as the sunflowers
that line the road to her grandparents' farm.
It's time to get ready for the reunion.
The horse nickers and chomps as Kara
feeds him carrots.

Laughter and tempting smells from the
kitchen fill the house.

Everyone makes welcome signs while Kara's
dad hangs the family tree.

All that's left is for tomorrow to come.

The next day, Amanda's family passes tipi rings visible on the golden prairie. The sacred round outlines hold the earth—a reminder of their ancestors and that they are almost home.

They turn off the highway onto the rutted dirt road. Amanda finally sees the family farm and hugs her doll tighter.

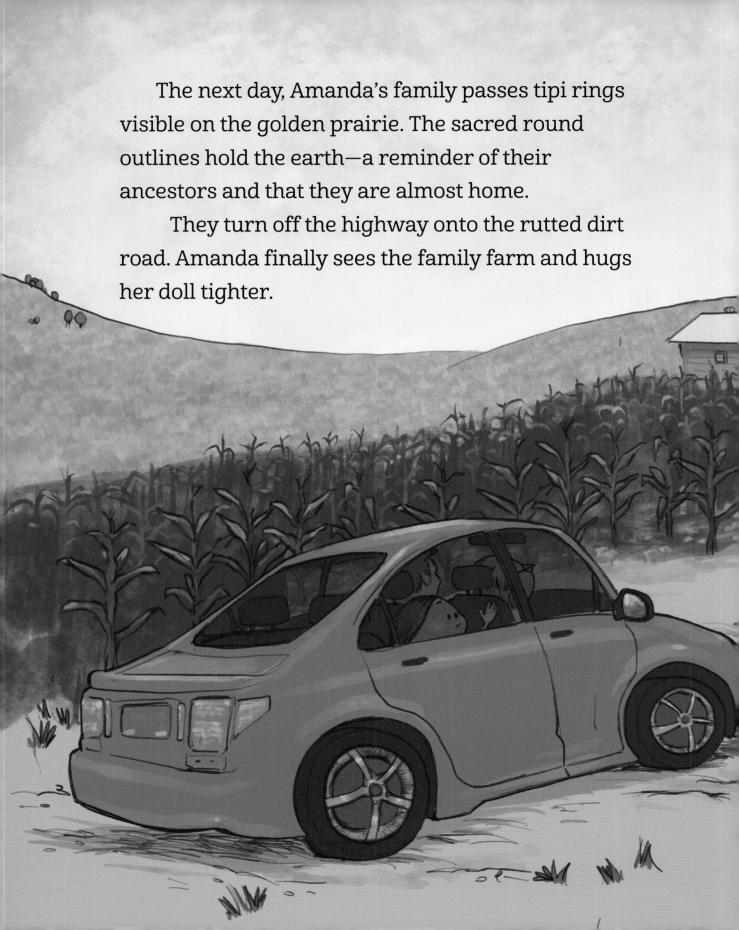

Kara is busy putting up signs. She spies
Amanda's car pulling up and hugs her doll tighter.

"Amanda, are you okay?" asks her mama.

"Fine," she says quickly.

Will Kara be happy to see me? Amanda wonders.

"Kara, can I help you with that sign?"
asks her mama.

"I've got it, Mama," she says, shrugging.

Will Amanda be happy to see me? Kara wonders.

The reunion begins with big hugs and hellos
and introducing the new baby.
The reunion also begins with two shy cousins.

Then Forrest runs off with Kara's and Amanda's dolls and hides behind a big round hay bale.

Amanda goes to the left, while Kara rounds to the right.

Gotcha!

They giggle as Forrest runs away.
The cousins look down, and
their giggles grow quiet.

Then Amanda says quickly,
"I missed you so much."
"Me, too!" Kara exclaims.

Now it's like nothing has changed. The girls share secrets in the loft,

play tag in the cornfield,

and jump off logs to swim in the lake.

On the last day, the family has a ceremony.
There is the scent of sweetgrass and
burning sage.

There is the beat of the drum in an ancient song.
Magúu explains relationships.
And the new baby gets his Hidatsa name.

Amanda doesn't want to say goodbye again.
Kara takes Amanda's hand and thinks, *I don't want her to go.*

The car is packed once again.
The miles are many between the Rez and the city.
Everyday giggles and secret whispers will soon end.

Amanda says, "Here. You take my doll."

"And you take mine. I'll visit you next time," says Kara.

They are forever cousins.

COUSINS, COMMUNITY, CULTURE, AND CONNECTIONS

Amanda, Kara, and Forrest represent the many cousins my sister and I grew up with in the 1960s and '70s in California's Bay Area suburbs, which we called "the city." We are an intertribal Native American family, meaning that we come from different Native tribes. My parents were born in their traditional tribal homelands. They were surrounded by and had the support of their family and fellow tribal members. They had a deep connection to and love of their ancestral lands where their origin stories came from.

As we cousins grew up, our families would visit our home Reservations in the summer or for special occasions. "The Rez" is short for Reservation—and it's fun to say. The Reservations—lands of Tribal Nations—that we visited included Tsimshian community in Alaska; Tuscarora Nation in New York; Ohkay Owingeh Nation in New Mexico; Blackfeet Nation in Montana; and the Mandan, Hidatsa, and Arikara Nation in North Dakota. (There is a Hidatsa word in the story: *magúu* [mah-goo], which means *grandma*.)

As in the story, some of our cousins moved back to the Rez and some stayed in the city. The city and the Rez were both equally our home and community. As a matter of fact, we are dual citizens: first enrolled members of sovereign Tribal Nations and then citizens of the United States. The term "sovereign nation" means a Tribal Nation that governs itself. If it is federally recognized, then it has a governmental relationship with the United States as a nation within a nation. Reservations were created when Native Nations were promised goods and services in return for land, first by colonists and settlers and then by the US government. The promises made to Indigenous peoples were almost never upheld.

Like Kara and Amanda in the story, my cousins and I maintained close relationships even when we were far apart, because we shared similar family and tribal values (ideas about what is important to our family and how we should live). We had ceremonies to reinforce our culture, storytelling to explain our history, special cultural events such as powwows, and a large family that connected us all. We practiced cultural activities in the city or at home within our Tribal Nations that made us all feel connected no matter where we lived.

FROM THE RESERVATION TO THE CITY

My parents moved from the Reservation to the city as the result of the federal Indian Relocation Act of 1956, pitched as vocational job training. In actuality, the federal government wanted to erase Native culture by moving Native people to cities so they would adapt to the lifestyles of white people (called "assimilation"). This policy resulted in few job opportunities, poverty, and the overall loss of cultural support for many individuals and families. As of the 2010 census, 78 percent of us live away from our Reservations or tribal homelands.

My mom and dad were young, single, and recent graduates of the Haskell Institute, a post-high school vocational and business institution in Lawrence, Kansas (now Haskell Indian Nations University), so they were ready for an adventure and applied to the federal relocation program. Because my parents and their siblings graduated from Haskell with trade skills, they were able to find employment or continue college in the city. But the government's promise of job training went unfulfilled for most tribal people. Unfortunately, many families who moved to cities faced discrimination and racism. Luckily my parents had a Haskell Alumni Association club in the Bay Area, where they found a group of intertribal friends to lean on.

The treatment of Native Americans in the United States was and sometimes still is despicable. But as with the family in this story and with my own family, unjust experiences forge tight bonds between us and make us strong. Our resiliency is rooted in our ceremonies and culture. We have a deep love of home. The land reminds us of our ancestors, storytelling helps us make good decisions, and we continue to have love and loyal family connections that are unbreakable.

FOR MY MOTHER, SISTER, AND ALL MY FOREVER COUSINS—L. G.

FOR MY SON, NEPHEWS, AND NIECES—J. N.

Published by Charlesbridge
9 Galen Street
Watertown, MA 02472
(617) 926-0329
www.charlesbridge.com

Library of Congress Cataloging-in-Publication Data
Names: Goodluck, Laurel, author. | Nelson, Jonathan (Illustrator)
  Illustrator.
Title: Forever cousins / Laurel Goodluck; Illustrated by Jonathan Nelson.
Description: Watertown, MA: Charlesbridge, [2022] | Audience: Ages 4–7. |
  Audience: Grades K–1. | Summary: Amanda and Kara are cousins and best
  friends in an intertribal Native American family; but Kara's family
  leaves the city and moves back to the Rez, making both girls sad—but
  the summer reunion reminds them that they will always be cousins.
Identifiers: LCCN 2021013872 (print) | LCCN 2021013873 (ebook) |
  ISBN 9781623542924 (hardcover) | ISBN 9781632899262 (ebook)
Subjects: LCSH: Indians of North America—Juvenile fiction. |
  Cousins—Juvenile fiction. | Best friends—Juvenile fiction. | Moving,
  Household—Juvenile fiction. | CYAC: Indians of North America—Fiction.
  | Indian reservations—Fiction. | Cousins—Fiction. | Best
  friends—Fiction. | Friendship—Fiction. | Moving, Household—Fiction.
Classification: LCC PZ7.1.G6539 Fo 2022 (print) | LCC PZ7.1.G6539 (ebook)
  | DDC [E]—dc23
LC record available at https://lccn.loc.gov/2021013872
LC ebook record available at https://lccn.loc.gov/2021013873

Printed in China
(hc) 10 9 8 7 6 5 4 3

Illustrations created digitally
Display type set in Canvas Curly by Ryan Martinson
Text type set in Cabrito by by Jeremy Dooley
Printed by 1010 Printing International Limited in
 Huizhou, Guangdong, China
Production supervision by Mira Kennedy
Designed by Diane M. Earley and Kristen Nobles